BRIDGE TO TERABITHIA

THE OFFICIAL MOVIE COMPANION

DAVID PATERSON

HarperEntertainment

A Division of HarperCollinsPublishers

For Lisa
thank you for your gift
which will last generations

As you will soon learn, my book *Bridge to Terabithia*, which is dedicated to my son David and to his friend Lisa Hill, is their story as well as mine. David has grown up to be a playwright and a screenwriter, and when he asked about turning the book into a film, I agreed at once. Neither of us could have imagined how difficult that would be. For years the major studios he approached told him the public wasn't interested in films made from children's books. Producers who were interested didn't have the money that the making of a major film requires. So it has taken many years and a shift in public attitude to make this film possible at all.

I remember years ago saying to David that, to succeed as a writer, he needed both talent and perseverance. I knew he had plenty of talent, but, then, the world is full of talented people. However, in the modern world, perseverance is in short supply. Only time would tell if he had that.

Well, time has proved to me that he has both. Turning the book *Bridge to Terabithia* into a movie has demanded gigantic portions of both talent and perseverance. Just writing the original script for the movie forced David to relive the great tragedy of his childhood. He has not only done that, he has worked tirelessly for years in his effort to help turn his script into a movie that will honor the spirit of the story.

On the following pages he will share with you, the reader, that long and painful journey, from grieving child to imaginative and compassionate writer and producer. Needless to say, his mother is very proud.

Katherine Paterson
Barre, Vermont

5

"What if the only way you could enter it is by swinging on this enchanted rope?"

—the movie script

What is Terabithia? It's something every kid should have. Have you ever felt lonely? Like you don't fit in? Like your parents are too busy to really notice you? Then what you need is a good friend and a place like Terabithia, the magical kingdom dreamed up by Jess Aarons and Leslie Burke.

In Terabithia, Jess and Leslie are the king and queen. They rule a magical empire! They fight terrifying monsters! And they form a friendship that will never end.

In Terabithia, anything is possible. It's a land of imagination, wonder, and hope.

▲ Jess's map of the land he and Leslie rule.

6

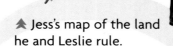
" 'We need a place,' she said, 'just for us.' "

▶ The king and queen of Terabithia plan their kingdom's future.

◀ In the book, Terabithia was created in the minds and hearts of two friends. But for the movie it took a large group of people to bring that magical land to life, including the director, cast, and crew.

David's Journal

Where is Terabithia?

Terabithia is that place in your heart
you go to feel safe, strong, and proud.
Terabithia is not necessarily a world,
but rather a state of mind. In the novel
it's a place where Jess feels confident;
it's a place where Leslie feels
appreciated. It is a place where they
can escape their everyday fears and
disappointments. It is, simply put, a
place of joy.

Jesse Oliver Aarons, Jr.

Jess Aarons is always running.

Jess is the only boy in his family. He's got two bossy older sisters and two whiny younger ones. His parents are too busy earning a living to pay him much attention. At school his teachers don't really notice him—he's just another ordinary kid. Nobody sees that he's a great artist. And Jess doesn't tell anyone. People wouldn't understand.

On the first day of school, Jess plans to show up everybody. He's been practicing all summer to become the fastest runner in the school. But the new kid beats him in a race. Even worse, she's a girl!

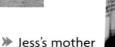

« Money's tight in Jess's family. Everyone has chores.

» Jess's mother and sisters.

» Jess helps out in the greenhouse.

▲ Jess's parents.

David's Journal

Jess longs for warmth from his dad, a man of few words and even fewer emotions. Jess is desperately in need of someone, anyone, he can call a friend.

Jess makes sure no one at school sees his artwork.

Jess has to sit next to Gary Fulcher, a school bully.

"He had to be the fastest—not one of the fastest or next to the fastest, but *the* fastest. The very best."

Leslie Burke

▲ Leslie and Jess each need a friend.

➤ Leslie's parents encourage her to be creative.

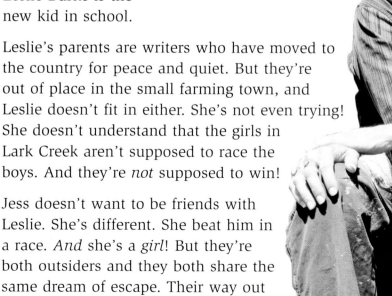

Leslie Burke is the new kid in school.

Leslie's parents are writers who have moved to the country for peace and quiet. But they're out of place in the small farming town, and Leslie doesn't fit in either. She's not even trying! She doesn't understand that the girls in Lark Creek aren't supposed to race the boys. And they're *not* supposed to win!

Jess doesn't want to be friends with Leslie. She's different. She beat him in a race. *And* she's a *girl*! But they're both outsiders and they both share the same dream of escape. Their way out becomes Terabithia.

⩔ Leslie's fast on her feet.

» With her loud clothes and her bright ideas, Leslie's not afraid to stand out.

▲ At home with Brenda, Ellie, and May Belle.

▲ Getting wet!

▲ Jess often hides his drawings.

➤ Jess tries to keep the school bullies from noticing him.

It would have been easy for Jess to hate Leslie. But he can't help seeing something special in her, even if the other kids think she's weird. When Leslie reads an essay on SCUBA diving, Jess feels like he's swimming underwater, too. On the school bus, Leslie sits in the seat "reserved" for Janice Avery, the eighth grade bully. He's got to warn her! By the end of the ride it looks like Leslie and Jess aren't going to be enemies after all.

◀ On your mark . . . get set . . .

▼ . . . go!

▲ Janice Avery charges Leslie a dollar to use the bathroom.

▲ Music class with beautiful Ms. Edmunds is the best part of school for Jess.

▲ Does Leslie really know how to SCUBA dive?

▲ Scott Hoager and Gary Fulcher always pick on Jess.

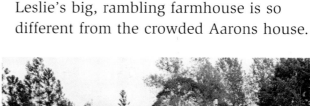

Leslie's big, rambling farmhouse is so different from the crowded Aarons house.

13

"She ran as though it was her nature."

David's Journal

Leslie offers Jess something he's never had before—friendship. And it's not just companionship—she listens to him, giving him an opportunity to express his emotions and frustrations without judging him.

▲ "Um, I don't know this game."
"What *game*? This is for real!"

◀ Leslie and Jess on their way to Terabithia.

"Somebody long forgotten had hung a rope."

Leslie swings across a creek on an old rope hanging from a tree. Jess follows her. And they land in Terabithia!

Terabithia is a secret kingdom, full of creatures that spring from Leslie's and Jess's imaginations. The Dark Master roams the woods, and the jangle of his prison keys lets them know of his approach. Squogres drop pinecone grenades. Hairy Vultures swoop down. Leslie and Jess turn an old tree house into a fortress. They're the king and queen of Terabithia.

David's Journal

Leslie shows Jess that the imagination is something to be proud of, a valuable gift that can be limitless.

≪ A fortress for
the king and queen.

▲ "Close your eyes. But keep
your mind WIDE OPEN."

▲ Squogres and Hairy Vultures remind Leslie and Jess
of the bullies at school.

▲ "C'mon, you can see the
whole kingdom from here!"

Back in real life, Janice Avery gets Jess thrown
off the school bus and squirts ketchup over
Leslie's face and hair. For his birthday, Jess
receives a car racetrack from his family and
something even better from Leslie, an art set.

But no matter what happens at home or school,
Terabithia is always waiting for Jess and Leslie.

≪ Happy birthday to Jess!

⩔ Trapping a troublesome garden intruder.

▲ Jess tries out his birthday gift.

▲ On the bus. Jess and Leslie would rather be in Terabithia!

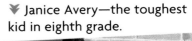
▼ Janice Avery—the toughest kid in eighth grade.

▲ Jess helps out Ms. Edmunds, his favorite teacher.

▲ May Belle learns not to show off around Janice.

"He grabbed the end of the rope and swung out toward the other bank with a kind of wild exhilaration and landed gently on his feet, taller and stronger and wiser in that mysterious land."

▼ Free the pee! The revolt against Janice Avery.

▲ The footprints of the Giant Troll.

➤ The king, queen, and prince of Terabithia.

➤ The Dark Master sends the Giant Troll to terrorize Terabithia.

Janice Avery steals cake from May Belle's lunch, and May Belle expects her big brother, Jess, to make things right. But what can he do? Leslie's on May Belle's side. She refuses to pay Janice a dollar to use the bathroom, and she gets the first graders to back her up. "Free the pee!" they chant. But Jess knows that fighting Janice will only get him in trouble. He backs down.

Meanwhile a Giant Troll stalks Terabithia. Leslie and Jess need help from Prince Terrien, Giant Troll Hunter Extraordinaire. The puppy is Jess's gift to Leslie, and he discovers the Giant Troll's weak point.

Janice Avery has a weak point, too. Jess and Leslie make up a love note and sneak it into Janice's desk. When Janice believes that Willard Hughes really likes her, she's embarrassed in front of the whole school.

➤ Jess pitches in to help paint the Burkes' living room gold.

▲ The king and queen share a quiet moment in their kingdom.

▲ Swinging across the rushing water.

◄ Rain can't keep Jess and Leslie from Terabithia.

Jess and Leslie get their revenge on Janice. But when Leslie hears Janice crying in the bathroom, she discovers that Janice has more trouble in her life than they ever realized.

Jess has a problem, too—he's lost his father's keys, and (thanks to May Belle) they end up in Terabithia. A fierce battle between good and evil begins. But it turns out that the Giant Troll—just like Janice Avery—isn't quite as bad as everybody thought.

Jess and Leslie have always shared everything about Terabithia. But when Jess's favorite teacher takes him to an art museum for the day, he doesn't invite Leslie to come. With Jess gone, Leslie makes her own way to Terabithia.

▲ "My *keys*, Jess. You never gave them back."

◄ Leslie is surprised by the beauty of the church service.

"They'll be out in force."
"Who will?"
"Our *enemies*! You *need* me, Jess!"

"You can do it. Just keep looking up!"

Leslie and P.T. leave Terabithia.

19

Jess loves looking at art with Ms. Edmunds.

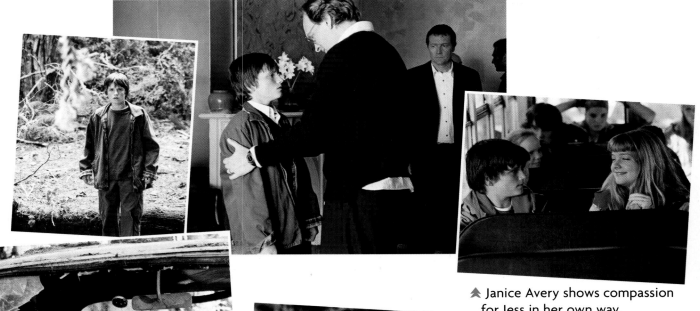

▲ Janice Avery shows compassion for Jess in her own way.

◄◄ Worried about Jess, May Belle follows him into Terabithia.

▲ Jess can't find the magic of Terabithia without Leslie.

Jess returns from the museum to hear heartbreaking news. When Leslie swung across the rushing creek into Terabithia, the old rope broke. Leslie drowned.

Jess's grief almost crushes him. But with the support of many people—including his normally abrasive teacher, his surprisingly tender father, and even Janice Avery—Jess starts to heal. He decides he *will* go to Terabithia again—but not alone. Jess shares the gift of imagination with his little sister May Belle. He even makes her a crown so that she can be the new princess of Terabithia.

▲ "And I wasn't here to go with her. It's all my fault!"

David's Journal

Life can be cruel sometimes, and very unfair. But the story does not end when Jess loses Leslie. The lessons Leslie taught Jess will be with him forever. She showed him the power of courage, the power of imagination, and the power of love and compassion.

▲ A simple request.

▲ A father and son connect.

➤ Jess's memorial for Leslie.

"Leslie was more than his friend. She was his other, more exciting self— his way to Terabithia and all the worlds beyond."

➤ Leslie's father agrees to let Jess have some old lumber . . .

▲ . . . perfect to make a bridge for the new princess of Terabithia.

New Zealand

Bridge to Terabithia is set in Lark Creek, a small town somewhere in the southern United States. So why was the movie filmed in New Zealand—halfway around the world?

The forests of Auckland, New Zealand, were perfect for the wilderness in which Jess and Leslie create the imaginary world of Terabithia. And New Zealand is home to Weta Digital. The people who worked for Weta would bring the creatures of Terabithia to life.

Some of the actors—such as Ema Feinton and Devon Wood, who play Jess's sisters—were from New Zealand. (They had to practice their American accents for the movie.) But AnnaSophia Robb, who plays Leslie, and Josh Hutcherson, who plays Jess, made the long trip from the United States to New Zealand to start turning *Bridge to Terabithia* from a book to a movie.

22

"*We scouted New Zealand to find a beautiful forest that these kids can discover.*"

—Hal Lieberman, producer

➤ The wild forests of New Zealand—a backdrop for vivid fantasies about Terabithia.

➤ Jess and Leslie on their way into their kingdom.

New Zealand is a beautiful country located east of Australia.

David's Journal

The natural beauty of the New Zealand countryside and woods added a magical quality that you could never capture on a Hollywood set.

Costume Design

« » The monsters of Terabithia are designed to remind people of the bullies who torment Jess. A Squogre wears an armband, a necklace, and a silver earring—just like Scott Hoager. Hairy Vultures look like Gary Fulcher.

Clothing can tell you a lot about a movie character. Everything from Jess's worn-out sneakers to Leslie's unique high-tops gives you hints about what they're like!

In the book, published in 1977, Leslie shows up on the first day of school wearing cutoffs and a T-shirt. That would have been a big deal in a small farming town back then. But, for the movie, Leslie's style needed an update. Her costumes were designed to be outrageous and to look as if she might have made some of them herself. "It's very funky, breaks the rules completely," AnnaSophia Robb, who plays Leslie, says. "Leslie is who she is. And she's not afraid to show it."

⩔ Leslie's parents wear funky clothes, too—just like their daughter.

▲ Leslie's fashion sense!

Among the first things you see of Jess in the movie are his shoes. The worn-out sneakers reveal a lot about him. He works hard. He's determined. And his family doesn't have money for fancy clothes.

➤ The Dark Master, the villain of Terabithia, has keys that sound like Jess's dad's work keys.

The Director

"I hope ultimately to reach and touch the audience's hearts by showing the transforming power and legacy of friendship. That is my biggest goal with this movie."

—Gabor Csupo, director

26

Gabor Csupo is the director of *Bridge to Terabithia*. He had worked on animated films before, but *Bridge to Terabithia* was his first movie where he directed live people.

"Gabor is so awesome," says Josh Hutcherson, who plays Jess. "He has the biggest heart of any director I think I've ever worked with, and he is just so caring; he's so nice."

"I really like his accent," adds AnnaSophia Robb, who plays Leslie. "He's Hungarian, so it's fun to listen to him."

Gabor wanted to make a movie that shows a balance between real life and the power of imagination. Terabithia is more than where Jess and Leslie go to escape—it's where they confront their problems and come up with ways to solve them. (Of course, it's also fun for a director to create a magical fantasyland. Gabor's favorite Terabithian character is the Giant Troll.)

But mostly Gabor believes that *Bridge to Terabithia* is about the journey of Jess's soul. The most important thing for Jess, Gabor says, "is passing on this beautiful legacy and love and the soulfulness that this little girl left behind."

In addition to Gabor, the director of photography, Michael Chapman, is responsible for the film's beautiful, dreamy visual look and feel.

Weta Digital

HOW THE MAGIC COMES TO LIFE!

Weta Digital in Wellington, New Zealand, creates digital effects for movies—everything from monsters or animals to entire cities! If you've seen King Kong on top of the Empire State Building or met Gollum in *The Lord of the Rings*, you've seen some of Weta Digital's work.

For *Bridge to Terabithia*, Weta Digital has created Squogres, Hairy Vultures, and the Giant Troll as well as Terabithia's forces of good: tiny Insect Warriors from the Treetop Provinces.

The very talented computer wizards at Weta Digital spend months bringing these creatures to life.

So when you see Jess and Leslie dodging Squogres or running from the Giant Troll, they're not actually seeing any creatures! Sometimes a person holds up a tennis ball on a stick to show them where to look.

THE SQUOGRE

THE INSECT WARRIOR

Stage 1: Production concept design

Stage 2: Weta Digital concept design for the Insect Warrior

Stage 3: Weta Digital concept design for the armor

Stage 4: 3-D model

Stage 5: Rendered 3-D Insect Warrior

THE SQUOGRE

Stage 1: Production concept design

Stage 2: Weta Digital concept design

Stage 3: 3-D model

Stage 4: Rendered 3-D Squogre

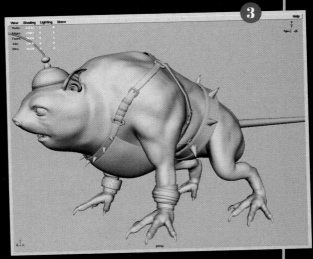

THE SQUOGRE

"They're miracle workers, alchemists, geniuses."

—Lauren Levine, producer

Jesse Oliver Aarons, Jr.
Josh Hutcherson

Thirteen-year-old Josh plays shy Jess Aarons, the main character in *Bridge to Terabithia*. The role of Jess is a big one—he's in nearly every scene. The movie needed a young actor with lots of experience. Luckily, Josh had already been in quite a few movies, including *Little Manhattan* and *Zathura*. One of the producers of the movie calls Josh "the can't-miss kid." "He's true to his character in every frame of the movie," he says.

30

▶ David Paterson with AnnaSophia and Josh.

"She's soulful and pretty and fun and she's the one that captures this boy's imagination and spirit and lets it soar."

—Hal Lieberman, producer

31

Leslie Burke
AnnaSophia Robb

AnnaSophia was cast early as smart, imaginative, courageous Leslie Burke. With several movies already to her credit, such as *Because of Winn-Dixie* and *Charlie and the Chocolate Factory*, she was eager to appear in *Bridge to Terabithia*. She loves the book and the character of Leslie. "She's always lit," AnnaSophia says. "She always has this happiness and glow about her." AnnaSophia also loves Leslie's clothes. "I want to take all of the clothes home," she says. "They're so cool!"

The Aarons
Robert Patrick and Katie Butler

Robert Patrick is the actor who plays Jess's father in the film, a man who doesn't talk much to his son but who loves him more than Jess realizes. Katie Butler played Jess's mother. She calls the movie "a story about friendship and loss and family and love."

Ms. Edmunds
Zooey Deschanel

Zooey Deschanel plays Ms. Edmunds, the beautiful music teacher who encourages Jess's passion for art. (Jess has a big crush on Ms. Edmunds!) Deschanel loved *Bridge to Terabithia* when she read it as a child, so she was excited to act in the movie.

Gary Fulcher
Elliot Lawless

Elliot Lawless plays Gary Fulcher, one of the school bullies who is always picking on Jess—and who is the inspiration for the Hairy Vultures of Terabithia. Elliot lives in Auckland, New Zealand.

Janice Avery
Lauren Clinton

Lauren Clinton plays the eighth grade bully. But there's more to Janice than meets the eye. Can Leslie befriend her? Lauren started acting at nine years old. She lives in Southern California with her parents, her brother, a Dalmatian, and a great big cat.

The Burkes
Latham Gaines and Judy McIntosh

Latham Gaines and Judy McIntosh play Leslie's creative parents. "A little wacky, but very fun and loving" is how Latham Gaines describes their on-screen family. Both actors live in New Zealand.

May Belle Aarons
Bailee Madison

Six years old, Bailee Madison plays May Belle Aarons, the little sister Jess never has time to play with. By the end of the movie, she walks across the bridge Jess has built to become the new princess of Terabithia.

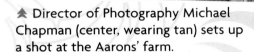

⌃ Director of Photography Michael Chapman (center, wearing tan) sets up a shot at the Aarons' farm.

⩔ We needed rain for this scene with Jess—so we made some!

Producers David Paterson, Lauren Levine, and Hal Lieberman, along with director Gabor Csupo, and many others, worked hard to bring *Bridge to Terabithia* to life in the movie. "It's a huge responsibility to adapt a book into a movie," says Lauren. "We had many 'gulp' moments as we expanded the story to make it as visually exciting as possible."

"The goal of our work was to honor and respect the power of Katherine Paterson's novel," says Hal. "We tried to keep our sensibilities aligned with the novel so that we delivered—through the script, and the cast, and in every way possible—what the book has to say and how it makes you feel."

34

⟨ It looks as if Jess is running alone. But actually there's a whole crew there, too!

≫ An everyday school bus—with a few extras.

SCHOOL BUS

STOP

LARK CREEK SCHOOL

FADE IN ON:

1   EXT. FIELD - SUNNY MORNING
    A boy FLASHES PAST, running full tilt, arms pumping, che
    heaving.

    CLOSE ON HIS FEET
    His beat-up sneakers, pounding the ground. One sole fla
    separating.

2   EXT. ROAD - CLOUDY DAY
    Same boy, different clothes, in a three-point stance by
    rural mailbox. As the MAIL TRUCK pulls off, he sprint
    alongside, racing it. The MAILMAN waves a hand out th
    window as he pulls ahead.

    CLOSE ON THOSE FEET
    That sole repaired with duct tape wrapped around the t

                                3

    EXT. FIELD -RAINY DAY   res finally coming into

▲ Waiting for filming to begin.

▲ AnnaSophia takes a swing.

▲ AnnaSophia with her stunt double. AnnaSophia's stunt double is actually a boy wearing a blond wig!

▲ A big smile for the camera.

The actors learn their lines and the cameras start rolling—right? Actually, shooting a scene in a movie is a little more complicated than that! Here's how you do it:

1) Make a storyboard—sketches to show what shots will be needed.

2) Create a previz, or previsualization. That's a bit like an animated cartoon made from the storyboard sketches. It gives you an idea of what the scene will look like.

3) While the actors are getting into costume and makeup, the director, the stunt supervisor, and the special effects people get together to talk about how to shoot the scene.

4) Have the crew position and set up the camera and sound equipment.

5) Bring in the actors. They walk through the scene and practice any special moves (such as battling Squogres).

6) Turn on the cameras! At last filming can begin.

◀ Director Gabor Csupo tells AnnaSophia and Josh what to do in the next scene. Often, actors have to repeat a scene while the director tries different camera angles or asks them to speak their lines in a new way.

AnnaSophia, Josh, and the other kids who acted in *Bridge to Terabithia* worked hard at the movie. But that doesn't mean they got out of going to school! They either went to small classrooms on the movie set or worked by themselves with tutors. Josh's and AnnaSophia's families came with them to New Zealand and rented houses where they stayed.

⏶ The only actor who never spoke a line was Paddy, who played the puppy, Prince Terrien.

When they weren't working or studying, the children found ways to have fun—painting, playing sports, or exploring the beautiful landscape of New Zealand.

 ⏵ Several cameras on one actor.

 Leslie "loves her parents because they're so creative," says AnnaSophia. "But she doesn't get attention from them, because they're always busy writing."

⏶ Making a movie isn't all hard work for Bailee Madison, the youngest actor on the set.

39

▼ Paddy, another star of Terabithia.

▲ Josh, holding Paddy, watches as his stunt double gets ready to swing across the creek.

▲ Waiting to shoot the next scene.

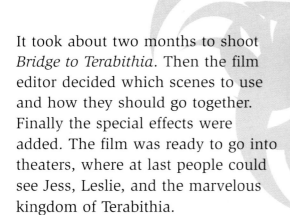

➤ Loosening up before a day of hard work.

It took about two months to shoot *Bridge to Terabithia*. Then the film editor decided which scenes to use and how they should go together. Finally the special effects were added. The film was ready to go into theaters, where at last people could see Jess, Leslie, and the marvelous kingdom of Terabithia.

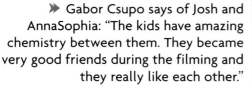

➤ Gabor Csupo says of Josh and AnnaSophia: "The kids have amazing chemistry between them. They became very good friends during the filming and they really like each other."

» The fortress in Terabithia belongs only to Jess and Leslie—but Josh and AnnaSophia have to share it with cameras, microphones, and many people!

¥ Lauren Clinton plays Janice Avery, a bully in the book and on the screen—but that doesn't mean that she and the other actors don't all get along in real life.

I wrote this book
for my son
David Lord Paterson,
but after he read it
he asked me to put Lisa's name
on this page as well,
and so I do.
For David Paterson and Lisa Hill,
banzai

⬆ Dedication page from the book *Bridge to Terabithia*.

⬆ Young Lisa Hill.

David's Journal

When I was seven years old, something wonderful happened to me. I met my best friend.

When I was eight years old, something terrible happened to me. My best friend, really, my only friend, died.

Her name was Lisa Hill.

When people meet me today and learn about the connection between my life and *Bridge to Terabithia*, many times their response is, "Wow. You're the original Jess. That's cool."

They mean it in a positive way, but it's like seeing a scar on somebody and remarking that the scar looks cool. They don't understand the pain that caused it.

⌃ David Paterson as a boy.

« David Paterson with Josh Hutcherson—two Jesses together.

Lisa's Gift

▲ David Paterson with Bailee Madison, who plays Jess's little sister May Belle.

When people find out that Jess's story is based on my life, many of them wonder how much I'm like Jess. There are many similarities. Jess liked to draw and run, he had a difficult relationship with his father, he kept mostly to himself in school, he was in love with his music teacher, and his family was poor. I liked to draw and run, I was somewhat distant from my dad, I kept to myself at school, I was in love with my music teacher, and we were pretty darn poor.

I didn't grow up on a farm like Jess. My family lived just outside Washington, D.C. But there *was* a creek that Lisa and I played in—Rock Creek. Lisa didn't drown in Rock Creek, though. She was struck by lightning at a beach in the summer of 1974.

"It was up to him to pay back to the world in beauty and caring what Leslie had loaned him in vision and strength."

I have always felt a deep connection with Lisa Hill, and all of my efforts to make *Bridge to Terabithia* into a film are meant to be in her honor. Lisa's tragedy was responsible for the book and now this film. You see, gifts come in two forms. They are temporary like a rainbow or permanent like a diamond. Lisa was both. Even though Lisa was on this earth for such a short time, the impact of her life will touch millions of kids for years to come.

Lisa's gift to us is *Bridge to Terabithia*. It is a gift of the imagination; it is the gift of friendship. It is the gift of hope.

To Lisa Hill

Banzai

Josh Hutcherson and AnnaSophia Robb sharing the book that made their movie possible.

The Book That Built a Bridge

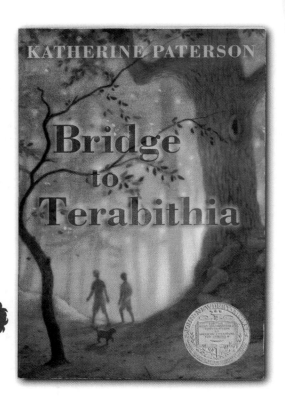

"In writing Bridge to Terabithia, *I was able to examine, at a deep level, a painful and frightening experience and emerge on the other side with a new sense of hope and joy."*

—Katherine Paterson

▲ The Newbery Medal is given each year to the author of "the most distinguished contribution to American literature for children." It's named for a bookseller from the eighteenth century, John Newbery.

When Katherine Paterson first wrote *Bridge to Terabithia* she was unsure how it would be received because of the sad events that occur in the book. But once her editor, Virginia Buckley, read the manuscript, she knew that it was so different, so honest, and so direct that it would be a book to be remembered. Some critics said children could not deal with the serious issues that are in the book, but Virginia knew kids could.

Katherine's editor was right. *Bridge to Terabithia* received the 1978 Newbery Medal, the most prestigious award in the U.S.A. for a children's novel. But that was only the beginning. In the thirty years since its publication it has been translated into more than twenty-five languages and won awards in Poland, Germany, the Netherlands, and France. Katherine receives letters from all over the world from people young and old who have brought the sad events of their own lives to her story and made it their own.

Now that *Bridge to Terabithia* is a movie as well, even more people can come to know Jess, Leslie, and Terabithia.

"We rule Terabithia! And no one can take that away!"

—the movie script

Bridge to Terabithia: The Official Movie Companion
Quotes from *Bridge to Terabithia* Copyright © 1977 by Katherine Paterson
Text Copyright © 2007 by David Paterson
Movie photographs © Copyright 2006 Walden Media, LLC. All rights reserved.
Movie artwork © Copyright 2006 Buena Vista Pictures Marketing and Walden Media, LLC. All rights reserved.
Weta Digital images © Walden Media, LLC. All rights reserved. Unit Photographer: Kirsty Griffin.
Images pages 28 and 29 courtesy of Weta Digital Ltd.
Photographs of Lisa Hill on page 42 used by permission of Inge Hill.
Photograph of David Paterson, age 8 (in sweater) on page 43 used by permission of David Paterson.
Cover art on page 46 Copyright © 2003 by Chris Sheban
Printed in the United States of America.